Quincy Rumpel
and the
Woolly Chaps

Quincy Rumpel
and the
Woolly Chaps

Betty Waterton

A Groundwood Book
Douglas & McIntyre
Toronto/Vancouver

The publisher gratefully acknowledges the assistance of the Ontario Arts Council
and the Canada Council.

Canadian Cataloguing in Publication Data

Waterton, Betty
   Quincy Rumpel and the woolly chaps

ISBN 0-88899-160-6

I. Title.

PS8595.A73Q44 1992 jC813'.54 C92-094027-7
PZ7.W38Qu 1992

Groundwood Books/Douglas & McIntyre Ltd.
585 Bloor Street West
Toronto, Ontario M6G 1K5

Design by Michael Solomon
Cover illustration by Eric Beddows

Printed and bound in Canada

To Karen and Jamie,
Carla, Josh, Bonnie
and Zachary

1

Quincy Rumpel was perched in the cherry tree, her long blue-jeaned legs twined upwards around a branch. Balanced on her stomach was a worn old book of poems, opened in the middle.

Closing the book, Quincy shut her eyes and began reciting in clear, ringing tones:

"My name is Ozymandias, king of kings:
Look on my works, ye Mighty, and despair!"

Suddenly, in the distance, a door slammed. Footsteps pounded across the Rumpels' backyard towards the cherry tree.

"Guess what?" shrieked a voice. "Quincy, this'll knock your socks off! *Guess what?*"

Quincy opened her eyes and peered down through the leaves.

"Now what?" she sighed.

Hopping up and down on the ground below was her brother, Morris, the youngest Rumpel. His pants were clinging precariously to his skinny hips, and the cowlick on top of his head was quivering with excitement.

Gathering his breath, he yelled, "Grandpa Rumpel's got cholesterol and we're going to move to Hawaii!"

"*Move?!!*" The branches of the cherry tree shook violently as Quincy untangled her legs and dropped to the ground. "If you're making this up, Morris Rumpel, you're going to be sorry."

"I'm not! I promise. I heard Mom and Dad talking just now, and they said we're going to go to Hawaii and grow pineapples. Where's Leah? Wait'll I tell her . . ."

Quincy jerked her thumb towards the back fence. "Over there by the Murphys', doing a painting." As Morris bounded away to find his sister, Quincy tucked her book under her arm and hitched up her jeans. "I'm going to find out what's going on around here," she muttered. Her pony-tail snapping briskly from side to side, she strode across the scraggly lawn to the house.

Her parents were nowhere in sight, but from upstairs came a faint murmur of voices. *That little sneak, Morris,* she thought. *He must have been listening outside their room.*

Leaning on the newel post, Quincy craned her neck towards the upstairs. *Darn, I can't make out a word . . .*

Suddenly she decided her hair needed fixing. Climbing the steps two at a time and making sure she missed the squeaky one third from the top, she made her way up to the top landing. Snatches of conversation were coming from behind her parents' bedroom door.

". . . Grandpa . . . serious . . ." came her father's rumbling voice. ". . . Hawaii . . . move . . . unlimited (mumble mumble) . . . ranch . . . pineapples . . ."

Moaning softly to herself, Quincy sank down in a heap on the top step. *Then it must be true! Grandpa is seriously sick, and we're moving to Hawaii to a pineapple ranch!*

Her mind reeling, she scurried back downstairs.

I need food, she thought. Detouring into the kitchen, she grabbed an apple from the fridge. Then she tottered into the living-room, where she collapsed onto the chesterfield.

She was lying there trying to sort out her thoughts when the front door flew open and Morris burst in. He was still breathless.

Behind him, in a cloud of turpentine fumes, came Leah, the middle Rumpel. Topped with a mushroom-shaped straw hat and engulfed in an old paint-spattered shirt of Mr. Rumpel's, she was all but unrecognizable as she staggered in. In one hand she clutched some brushes and a Black Magic chocolate box containing her oil paints. The other hand grasped a pickle jar half-filled with murky turpentine. Balanced between the pickle jar and her chin was a painting on a stretched canvas.

Dropping the brushes and paints onto the coffee table, Leah carefully disengaged her painting, then set down the pickle jar.

"Morris says Grandpa Rumpel is dying and we have to move to Hawaii." Her round blue eyes grew wide as she looked at her older sister. "Poor Grandpa! And poor Grandma . . ."

"If Grandpa dies, Grandma can come to Hawaii with us," said Morris. "Then maybe she would buy a surf board, and we could all use it . . ."

A stair squeaked. Quincy held her finger up to her lips. "Ssssshhh," she hissed. "They're coming!"

As Mr. and Mrs. Rumpel came into view, their three children watched them warily from below.

"Oh, good," grinned Mr. Rumpel. "You're all here. Have we got some news for you!" Plopping himself down at one end of the sagging blue velvet loveseat, he stretched his long legs out in front of him.

"It's sort of good news and bad," said Mrs. Rumpel, settling herself beside him. "Which do you want first?"

I don't believe it! thought Quincy. *How can they be so cheerful?*

"I think we know the bad news," she said.

"Grandpa's dying with cholesterol!" blurted out Morris.

Mrs. Rumpel looked shocked. "Good heavens, no! Wherever did you get that idea? His count is a little high and he has to cut down on his butter tarts again, but that's nothing new. The bad news is that we're moving."

"To a pineapple ranch in Hawaii!" cried Quincy. "I knew it! That's not *too* bad. What's the good news?"

"The good news is where we're moving to," said her father. "Rumpel Ranch!"

Quincy, Leah and Morris stared at their parents. "Not Hawaii?" they chorused.

"Of course not. Where do you children get these strange ideas?" Mrs. Rumpel looked puzzled. "Grandma and Grandpa are thinking about a trip there before her course starts, though."

"But we thought . . . but you said . . ." stammered Quincy. "What course?"

"Grandma's marine mammal course, at the university. She's always been interested in the sea. That's probably where you got your interest in goldfish, Morris. Of course, we Twistles have always had an affinity for water, too. Did I tell you about the time Aunt Fan was studying frogs at Lake Memphremagog—"

"Anyway," interrupted Mr. Rumpel, "Grandma and Grandpa Rumpel are moving to the city and we're taking over their ranch at Cranberry Corners. I'm going to plant the biggest apple orchard you ever saw. The opportunities are unlimited. Rumpel Ranch will be known far and wide as the home of fine apples!''

Fine apples? *Pine*apples? Quincy groaned. Morris had done it again.

2

For a few moments Quincy, Leah and Morris were silent, as the full impact of the news sank in.

"You mean, we're actually going to move away from here? To *Cranberry Corners*?" Quincy glared at her parents.

"Well, at least Grandpa's not dying," said Leah sternly. "You should be thankful for that, Quince."

"Oh, I am. But I never actually believe anything Morris says, anyway." Quincy turned her glare on her brother.

"But I was right about us moving," protested Morris. "And it's not so bad at Cranberry Corners. They've got a real skookum bake shop there that makes little lemon tarts, and the hardware store has all kinds of neat sports stuff. I had a good time when I went to Rumpel Ranch last year. Remember I rode Fireweed and rescued the falcons and helped Grandpa with the Wings of Icarus and—"

"How could we help but remember? You told us about it a hundred times," said Quincy. Then she turned to her father. "Just when exactly do we have to go, Dad?"

"Pretty soon, I hope. Grandma and Grandpa are anxious to move, but they can't just leave old Fireweed to fend for herself. So the sooner we get there, the better." Pulling a shiny brochure out of his shirt pocket, Mr. Rumpel began to study the farm machinery displayed in it.

Leah looked anxiously at her picture on the coffee table. "But what about the Under-Twelve Earthwatch Art Show at the library? It starts tomorrow, and the first prize is a hundred dollars!"

"Don't worry, dear. We'll wait till the end of the art show," said her mother, leaning over to inspect the speckled yellow painting with the red dot in the middle.

"You're supposed to look at oil paintings from a distance," Leah told her, propping the picture on top of the bookcase. Closing one eye, she stood back, facing it. "Like this, see?"

Her parents squinted at it dutifully. "It's, uh, nice and bright," said Mrs. Rumpel finally. "What is it, dear?"

"Can't you tell?" chuckled Mr. Rumpel. "It's scrambled eggs with a squirt of ketchup!" Leah gave him a withering glance.

"It's a picture of dandelions, Dad," said Quincy. "With a ladybug, I think. She's been watering a patch of them in the backyard for the past two weeks."

"I haven't actually been watering them. They've been getting watered by the Murphys, when they do their peas and beans," said Leah. "I call it *The Last Dandelions*. It's environmental. But now it's all smudged, and it's all Morris's fault for rushing me in, telling me Grandpa was dying . . ."

"I'm sure you can fix it before tomorrow," said Mrs. Rumpel.

"Maybe she can fix her painting, but how am I going to fix my *life*?" groaned Quincy. "Here I am, practically a teenager! Don't you know moving to Cranberry Corners could have a serious impact on a person my age? Have you even thought what this might do to Freddie?"

Mrs. Rumpel looked at her daughter in alarm. "Well, no. I hadn't, actually."

"Maybe you'd better tell him, Quince," said Leah.

"I will. I am. Right now, in fact!" Closing the door behind her, Quincy retreated into the front hall.

"Poor Quincy," said Leah. "She says Freddie almost sat with her at lunch, too, the last day of school. She took a whole bunch of brownies to lure him, but it didn't work. She ended up eating them all herself. That's why she broke out in spots last week."

"So that's what happened to all those brownies," said Mrs. Rumpel. Leaving her husband studying farm tractors, she went into the kitchen to start supper.

Leah followed her, lugging her painting gear. She had barely got her things set up on the kitchen table when Quincy stormed in.

"You didn't talk very long." Leah began scraping off little gobs of yellow paint with a paring knife.

Quincy's blue eyes glinted dangerously. "Do you know what that nerd said? He said—and I quote—'Send me a postcard with a moose on it.' Ha! He's got a hope!"

Leah dabbed more paint onto her picture. "Maybe he was in shock."

"A moose!" Quincy ranted on. "I'm moving a zillion k. away, and all he cares about is a *moose*?"

"Only 500," said Mrs. Rumpel. "Now, will you please get busy and help, Quincy? We need something to go with the cabbage-roll casserole. Maybe a two-bean salad."

"Mother, my life is shattered, and all you can talk about is *food*!"

Suddenly Leah threw down her brush and burst into tears. "It's ruined!" she sobbed. "Totally ruined!"

"Maybe we could get you some painting lessons in Cranberry Corners," said Mrs. Rumpel soothingly.

Leah brightened. "Do you think so? Oh, I'd love to take painting lessons."

"I always thought you wanted riding lessons," said Quincy.

16

"I do. But right now I want painting lessons."

"When we're living on a *ranch*?" cried Quincy. "Don't you want a horse? If I'm going to have to live in Cranberry Corners, I'm going to get a horse right away. Probably a great big black stallion."

"Maybe you could ride Fireweed," suggested Mrs. Rumpel.

"Mother! Fireweed is thirty years old! Grandpa won't let anybody ride her anymore. He says she's just ornamental now."

Just then the back door banged open. "I told the Murphys," announced Morris breathlessly. "And I told the people in the white house, and the people in the yellow house, and the people with the pink flamingos, too. Everybody's real excited that we're moving, but nobody cried or anything."

* * *

"Cold pork and beans?" Mr. Rumpel looked doubtfully at his plate as he ladled out a spoonful of brown mush from the cut-glass salad bowl.

"It's a two-bean salad," said Quincy. "Two cans of pork and beans."

3

Sniffing the cold beans, Morris quickly passed them on down the table. "Freddie doesn't know how lucky he is we're moving. If we stayed here Quincy would probably marry him, and then he'd have to eat stuff like this all the time."

"In your dreams!" snorted Quincy.

Morris picked at his casserole and ate five buns. Then, mumbling something that sounded vaguely like "skews," he scraped back his chair. "Gotta go and tell Chucky. Man! Will he be surprised!"

Mrs. Rumpel looked at the rejected rice, chopped cabbage and ground meat on Morris's plate. "Are you sure you've had enough?" she called after him. But Morris had gone. "He didn't eat very much," she said worriedly.

"Mom, you know he hates mixtures," said Quincy. "He'll make up for it later, believe me."

Mr. Rumpel reached for a second helping of casserole. "I'll bet you girls can't even imagine a three-hundred-tree orchard in bloom."

"Three hundred apple trees full of blossoms," murmured Leah, closing her eyes. "I can picture it now."

Quincy smacked her lips. "Three hundred trees full of crunchy apples . . ."

"Of course, they'll have to be planted first. We'll need a post-hole digger for that. One that attaches to a tractor," said Mr. Rumpel. "I've been reading about them in the catalogue. One is called the Earth Auger. It has a hydraulic motor drive with reverse, and interchangeable bits—"

"No Earth Auger." Mrs. Rumpel's voice was firm. "No tractor. No interchangeable bits. How come you never mentioned all these things before, Harvey?"

"I've just figured out how this equipment will pay for itself. Not only can we plant our apple trees with it and put up fences, but I can drill post holes for other people."

"Way to go, Dad," said Quincy. "You sure have it all figured out."

"There's no telling how many post holes I can dig up there. Why, I bet the whole country needs new post holes!" cried Mr. Rumpel. Jumping up from his chair, he began striding around the room, his hands clasped behind his back. "Between post holes and apple trees, the potential is unlimited. The Rumpel fortunes are on the rise at last!"

"If we're going to be rich," said Quincy, "maybe I can have two horses. Then I could lend one to my friends when they come to visit."

Leah stared at her. "How come you're suddenly so interested in horses? You never were before."

"We never lived on a ranch before, did we?"

Mr. Rumpel paused in his patrol of the kitchen. "We can't get any horses right away, you know, girls. Actually, it may be quite a while. Maybe after we harvest a crop or two of apples."

"Oh, well," said Leah. "I guess I can wait. I can always practise a few things on Fireweed, like grooming and cleaning tack, and things like that. Besides, I'll have my painting lessons to do this year."

"I can't wait," said Quincy. "I want a horse right away. I can earn my own money for it. I'll help Dad dig post holes."

"I'd like that, Quincy. But I'm a long way from hiring a ranch-hand, you know. Maybe next year."

"A ranch-hand! That's what I'll be! Somebody up there must need one of those. I'm plenty strong."

"But you haven't any experience, dear," said her mother.

"I mucked out Fireweed's stall, once."

Just then the door opened and Morris clumped back in. He looked hot and steamy. Kicking off his sneakers, he headed for the fridge and poured himself a glass of lemonade. "Chucky was out, so I ran all the way home. Man, am I ever sweating!"

"Phew!" Leah held her nose. "Mother, can't you make him wear socks in his sneakers?"

"Morris, as soon as you drink that, I want you to hop into the shower," ordered his mother.

"Aw, Mom. I'll get cramps. Like, how about when I go to bed?"

"Now! And leave your sneakers on the back porch. Which reminds me, I noticed a funny smell in your closet this morning. You'd better check it out."

"It's probably just my jellyfish. Me and Chucky rescued some at the beach last week, but they went all goopy-looking."

"I knew it!" cried Quincy. "I knew there was something dead in his room! Mother, when we move to the ranch, will you *please* put Morris out in the barn or somewhere? Anywhere but next to Leah and me. I'm really sick and tired of living beside him and all his smelly creatures."

Morris beamed. "Right on! I'd like to sleep in the barn."

"No. No barn." Mrs. Rumpel was adamant. "And you all know Grandma and Grandpa's house is small, so I'm afraid Morris will have to have the room next to you girls upstairs." Giving a sigh, she added, "There's just no other place to put him . . ."

4

Neither Leah nor Quincy could get to sleep that night. They lay in their beds, each girl thinking her own thoughts.

"It's all over, isn't it?" Quincy sighed at last. "Our life at 57 Tulip Street is all over. Farewell Aunt Ida, Uncle George and Cousin Gwen. Farewell Murphys. Farewell lovely beach, miserable school. Farewell forever, F.J. Twikenham. The Rumpels are about to take a quantum leap into the unknown . . ."

"Cranberry Corners isn't really *that* unknown," said Leah. "We've been there lots of times. But I'm worried about my painting, Quince. It's still wet and I shouldn't have left it in the kitchen. What if Morris sits on it when he goes down for one of his late-night snacks? I think I'll go and get it."

"Bring back some fig bars and oranges. Oh, and some garlic sausage and crackers."

Leah brushed her blonde hair and put a fuzzy pink dressing gown over her flowered nightie. Then she buttoned on her knitted pink slippers (from

Grandma Twistle last Christmas) and padded downstairs.

After punching her pillow into shape and putting on her glasses, Quincy sat up in bed, her arms clasped behind her head. Her green cotton night-shirt was decorated with Brussels sprouts, leeks, turnips and the words, *Free the Veggies*.

At last Leah shuffled back in, *The Last Dande-lions* in one hand and a plateful of food in the other. She deposited the plate on Quincy's bed and put the picture under her own.

"On the floor?" Quincy stuck some sausage on a cracker.

"It's not that I don't trust you or anything. I just don't want you to get crumbs on it. It's still tacky." Providing herself with some fig bars and an orange, Leah unbuttoned her slippers and climbed into bed.

* * *

The next morning, Quincy was wakened by a sort of yelp. Leah was on her hands and knees, hauling her picture out from under the bed.

"Look at it!" she wailed. "It's got fluff all over it!"

Quincy leaned over. "I thought that was kind of a dumb place to leave it. But not to worry. We can get it off."

"But there's no time! It has to be in by nine this morning!" cried Leah, picking frantically away at her painting.

"Tweezers." Quincy's voice was calm. "Just get me tweezers and a toothbrush."

"Whose toothbrush?"

"I don't care. We're not going to clean teeth with it. Get Morris's."

But by 8:45, *The Last Dandelions* was still covered in a faint whitish fuzz.

"I can't take it in like this!"

"Sure you can. I'll go with you. Maybe the rest will all fall off before we get there."

At 8:55, they set out for the library.

"This is so embarrassing," panted Leah as they scurried along the street. "Everybody's looking at my picture."

"You'll have to get used to that," said Quincy, "if you're going to be an artist."

5

"Oh, look at them all!" moaned Leah in dismay, as the two girls walked into the library.

Quincy glanced at the paintings stacked against the wall. There were pictures of trees being hugged and pictures of blue recycling boxes. One painting looked like a lumpy mattress with a hole in the middle. It was called "The Hole in the Ozone."

Hoo, boy, thought Quincy. *There sure are a lot.*

"At least your frame is nice," she whispered to Leah. "And your painting looks a lot better in it than that old picture of Aunt Fan swimming across Lake Memphremagog."

Clasping *The Last Dandelions* to her chest with both hands, Leah lined up to register.

"I'm going to look for a book," said Quincy. Leah nodded numbly.

Quincy ambled away. Spotting a woman carrying a stack of books, she quickened her pace and followed her into a back office, hissing, "Pssssssst! Psssssst!"

The librarian dropped all her books but one — a large and heavy one (The New, *New*, Changing World Atlas). Raising it threateningly over her head, she whirled around.

"Ranch-hands," whispered Quincy in a conspiratorial tone. "Have you got any good books on ranch-hands?"

The librarian put down her atlas. "Did you look under 'Careers'?"

Quincy grinned and winked. "Quelle bonne idée! Muchos gracias!" And she darted away.

Leah eventually found her sister leaning against some shelves, reading.

"I couldn't find anything about ranch-hands," Quincy told her. "But look what I found. It's called *Roxy the Range-Rider.*"

On the cover, a girl in sheepskin chaps and a wide-brimmed white cowboy hat appeared to be galloping towards some cows, her long braid of red hair streaming out behind.

"Don't you think she looks like me?" asked Quincy.

"Not much. Her hair's redder, and longer. And she's older. She looks about eighteen."

Quincy peered closely at the cover. "She might be. But she goes on cattle drives, and that's exactly what I want to do, so I'm taking it out."

At home, the girls took some snacks up to their room, flopped on their beds and began to read.

At first only munching and crunching noises broke the silence. Then Quincy cried, ''Just listen to this! 'A tangled clump of tumbleweed came rolling across the corral and fastened itself to Roxy's sheepskin chaps as the intrepid young range-rider leaped onto her horse and galloped off after the runaway herd.' Oh, man! Can't you just see her?''

''Some day I'm going to have a thoroughbred,'' sighed Leah. ''And do dressage. Or maybe I'll get an Arabian. They're *so* beautiful. Of course, they cost a lot, so I'll probably have to wait for years and years.''

''Well, I'm not waiting. I want a horse now. Just a nice, normal horse. A quarter-horse would be perfect. And I want to wear woolly chaps, like Roxy. And I want to go on trail rides and cattle drives and stuff.''

That night, in the middle of chicken and dumplings, Quincy made her announcement. ''I'm thinking of changing my name, everybody.''

Mrs. Rumpel's fork clattered to the floor. ''Change your name? To what? I thought you loved your name.''

''Oh, I do, Mom. I just think Roxy suits me better.''

* * *

The day after the closing of the Under-Twelve Earthwatch Art Show, the five Rumpels and their

27

hairy white dog, Snowflake, finally left for Cranberry Corners.

To everyone's surprise, Leah's painting had won third place in the Multi-media category. "The addition of texture to *The Last Dandelions*," said the judges, "shows the emergence of an exciting new talent."

The prize was a gift certificate at the drugstore, which Leah used to purchase ten dollars' worth of hair barrettes.

6

Mrs. Rumpel drove the station wagon, with Leah and Quincy in the front seat beside her. The back was piled higgledy-piggledy with pillows, lamp shades, boxes of Christmas tree ornaments, pots and pans, ski boots and a large rubber tree plant—Aunt Ida's parting gift. Also Mr. Rumpel's doorknob collection, Grandma Twistle's good china dinner set, Leah's painting and Quincy's stuffed animals. At the last minute, Morris decided to send his pet goldfish—Leonardo and Donatello. "It will be smoother for my little guys if they ride in the car," he said as he tucked them into the back seat.

Everything else went in the rent-a-truck with Mr. Rumpel, Morris and Snowflake.

As they careened around the corner at the end of their street, Mrs. Rumpel gazed towards the beach and sighed. "It's been lovely living so near the sea. I'm going to miss it."

"Me, too," snuffled Leah. "And I'll miss my friends, and my school, and my teacher, and my

Sunday School teacher, and the lady in the bake-shop, and—"

"Ha!" said Quincy. "I sure won't miss school. And I won't miss dear Cousin Gwen, and I certainly *won't* miss that twerp, Twikenham. But I'll miss the cherry tree . . . and goofing around on the beach . . . and Aunt Ida's dream cake. Actually, I think I'm probably much too mature for Freddie, now that I'm going to be a ranch-hand. I might even start my own business with a whole string of horses. I could call it 'Ride the Trails With Roxy.' "

As Mrs. Rumpel waited to merge onto the highway, Leah pointed out the window. "Look! There go Daddy and Morris!"

The yellow rent-a-truck lumbered past, tooting its horn, and the three Rumpels caught a fleeting glimpse of a white face peering out at them.

"Morris looks pale," said Mrs. Rumpel. "I hope he isn't going to be carsick again."

"That wasn't Morris, Mom," chorused Leah and Quincy. "That was Snowflake."

For a while the journey proceeded without incident. Then Quincy got hungry. Twisting around in her seat belt, she groped about in the back, trying to reach the picnic basket.

"Ouch! Ouch! Ow!" howled Leah. "Get your elbow out of my face!"

"Keep your face out of the way, then," grunted Quincy, undoing her seatbelt.

Hanging over the back of the seat, she managed to take the lid off the picnic basket. ''Mom, I can't feel any sandwiches in here.''

''That's because I didn't bring any,'' said Mrs. Rumpel. ''When did I have time to make sandwiches? There's cheese and crackers and apples.''

''I feel some jellied fruit salad in a plastic bag.''

''Oh, I'll bet Aunt Ida put it in. She said she was giving us a little treat for our trip.''

But a moment later an anguished cry came from behind the seat.

''OH, NO!''

As Leah turned around to look, Quincy's rear end heaved and wobbled. ''Help! This isn't jellied salad! It's Morris's goldfish! And that stupid Leonardo jiggled right out when I undid the twistie tie to see the salad. Now how can we ever find him in all this junk? Mom, you've got to stop the car.''

''Hurry, Mom! Stop the car!'' cried Leah.

''I'm trying to! I'm looking for a place to pull off . . .''

Leah pointed ahead. ''There's one! It says 'Emergency only.' ''

''Well, this is sure an emergency. Leonardo's a goner if we don't find him, like, fast,'' said Quincy, climbing over into the back.

''Watch out for the rubber tree!'' cried Mrs. Rumpel, swerving onto the gravel shoulder.

''I hear a siren,'' said Leah.

31

Mrs. Rumpel slammed on the brakes. "It's the police," she groaned.

The cruiser pulled in behind them and two Mounties got out and strode over. Before they had a chance to speak, Quincy poked her head up from behind the front seat.

"We haven't done anything, sirs! Except Mom ran a yellow light back in town, but that was just because we were trying to catch up with Daddy and Morris. They're in that rent-a-truck with the two garbage cans tied on behind . . ."

"We just wanted to ask if you're having trouble," said one of the Mounties.

"Oh, yes, sirs!" said Quincy. "We sure are. Leonardo's lost!"

"Morris will kill us!" moaned Leah.

The Mounties looked at each other. "Just who are these characters?" asked one, taking out his notebook. "This Morris. What's his last name?"

"Rimpel . . . Dumpel . . . I mean, Rumpel," stammered Mrs. Rumpel. "But don't write his name down. He's just a baby!"

"Just for the record, ma'am. Now, the missing one. Leonardo who?"

"He doesn't have a last name," said Leah.

"Description?" The policeman's pencil was poised over his notebook.

Quincy furrowed her brows. "Well, he's sort of mottled, with long black wavy whiskers and buggy eyes. Actually, he's a real mean-looking goldfish, but he's Morris's favourite, so I'd better find him.''

''Goldfish?'' The two Mounties rolled their eyes at each other. The one with the pencil and notebook put them back in his pocket.

''Well,'' he said, ''if he hasn't flipped out the window, we'll find him.''

Thirty seconds later Leonardo was discovered, his mouth open and his tail quivering weakly, in the bottom of one of Grandma Twistle's teacups.

''You rascal!'' cried Quincy. Scooping him up, she dumped him back into his plastic bag.

After advising Mrs. Rumpel that she had far too many stuffed toys in her rear window, the policemen returned to their car. Then they took off with a friendly wave and an official-sounding squeal of their tires.

7

"There it is!" Leah pointed ahead. "I see the Rumpel Ranch mailbox!"

"Thank goodness." Mrs. Rumpel breathed a sigh of relief. "I think I'm getting a headache."

Quincy had been chattering almost non-stop for the last few hours, retelling the saga of Roxy the Range-Rider. Now she was suddenly silent as she looked at the red, white and blue mailbox topped with a large red maple leaf. *This is ours now,* she thought. *Here it is, Quincy Rumpel—a new chapter in your life. From now on things will be very different. You will be very different. You will get a job, a horse, a pair of woolly chaps . . .*

"Hey, Mom! Look out! You nearly hit that bunny!"

"The bunnies will have to look after themselves today," said Mrs. Rumpel grimly, as she turned down a narrow dirt road. "I just want to get this trip over with."

They swerved around a bend and pulled up beside a smallish log house.

"Fireweed's eaten all of Grandma's geraniums again," said Leah, looking at the decapitated potted plants on the front porch.

The rent-a-truck was parked by the door. It was in the process of being unloaded by Mr. Rumpel, Grandpa and Grandma.

"What kept you?" Mr. Rumpel asked his wife.

"The goldfish. One of them got loose and—"

Just then Morris flew out of the house clutching a half-eaten triple-decker sandwich. "Which one?" he cried. "Not Leonardo, I hope!"

Quincy nodded.

"Oh, no!" Morris smacked his forehead with his sandwich. "Where is my little guy?"

"Don't worry. He's safe," said Quincy as Morris dived into the station wagon.

"We pulled over to look for Leonardo," explained Mrs. Rumpel. "And that was when the Mounties came."

Mr. Rumpel set down a laundry basket full of rubber boots. "How much?" he groaned.

"They didn't give us a fine, Dad," Quincy told him. "They thought we were in trouble because we were sort of in an Emergency Only area."

"Actually, they were very friendly," added Leah. "And they were the ones who found Leonardo in Grandma Twistle's teacup."

"He looks all funny around his face," said Morris, peering into the plastic bag. "And he's sort of bloated, too."

"He's probably just full," Quincy assured him. "I thought he might need something to eat after his teacup experience and I couldn't find any fish food, so I gave him some cracker crumbs. But I think you'd better get him into his aquarium pretty quick."

Morris disappeared inside, and the unloading continued. Afterwards everybody sat down to a welcome meal of baked ham, hot rolls, potato salad and Aunt Ida's dream cake (which had been located in a corner of the picnic basket).

"I didn't think she'd give us jellied salad in a plastic bag," said Mrs. Rumpel. "But you never know."

Just before dark, Grandma and Grandpa Rumpel climbed into their little red sports car. With their suitcases and their old black dog, Rocket, in the jump seat behind, they zoomed down the driveway, waving happily.

"What's that long thing sticking out the back?" wondered Leah.

"Oh, no!" groaned Morris. "That's the Wings of Icarus — Grandpa's hang glider. He's taking it with him. And I was planning to use it."

The five Rumpels strolled around inspecting their new property. They toured the chicken house, the workshop, the barn. They surveyed their grassy pasture and imagined how it would look all a-bloom with apple blossoms. They leaned on their wooden fence rail and gazed lovingly at their livestock — eleven chickens, and a very old horse.

Plucking a handful of grass, Quincy climbed over the fence. Fireweed raised her head. Eyeing the grass, she began plodding over.

Quincy rubbed the silky neck. "We all love you, Fireweed," she whispered. "Even if you are old and we can't ride you anymore."

Mr. Rumpel gazed dreamily at the barn. "Can't you just picture a little green tractor sitting there? I think maybe I'll take a look around town tomorrow, when we take the truck in . . ."

But Mrs. Rumpel's chin had just jutted out and her lips had tightened into a firm line.

"You're not spending the day looking at tractors," she said. "There are too many things that need doing around here." She pointed to the chickens stalking single-file towards the open back door. "Just look at them. They're headed for the kitchen!"

"They're free-range hens," said her husband. "They're used to being loose. But I suppose I could make them a run sometime."

"Can I come to town tomorrow with you?" asked Quincy. "I have to put up my signs."

"What signs?" asked Leah.

"My Employment Wanted signs. For my job. To make money so I can buy a horse."

"I need to get some goldfish medicine," said Morris.

"I want to see if they have painting lessons in Cranberry Corners," said Leah.

"And I have to get some groceries," said Mrs. Rumpel. "We may as well all go in. But right now what I want is a nice, hot bath."

The two girls were doing the dishes when Mrs. Rumpel padded into the kitchen wrapped in a Ninja Turtle beach towel. She did not look pleased.

"Where is your brother?" she cried.

"Out with Dad. Dad said they had to check fences," replied Quincy. "I thought you were going to have a bath."

"I *am* going to have a bath. I am going to have a big bath. I am going to have the biggest, hottest, bubbliest bath anybody in this family has ever had. Just as soon as somebody gets those two stupid goldfish out of the bathtub!"

8

In Cranberry Corners the next morning, Mrs. Rumpel was just coming out of the supermarket when she suddenly stopped short. Tacked to the telephone pole in front of the store was a notice, bordered with interlocking pink horseshoes:

AVAILABLE IMMEDIATELY!!!
Strong, athletic, horse-loving girl desperately needs work!!! Experienced rider!!! Dog trainer!!! TV personality!!!
Phone Quincy Rumpel, at Rumpel Ranch.

"Good grief!" exclaimed Mrs. Rumpel.

By the time the family met at the car to go home, all the Rumpels had seen Quincy's advertisements.

"*Athletic?*" cried Morris. "You mean pathetic!"

"I played volleyball at school last year."

"Experienced rider?" scoffed Leah. "That's a hoot!"

"I've ridden Fireweed."

"Once!"

"But a TV personality?" Mrs. Rumpel shook her head. "That's hardly true, Quincy."

"But, Mom! I was on TV. Don't you remember the school play when I was the minotaur and I helped advertise Rumpel Rebounders? I even made the ten o'clock news. Anyway, Dad said we sometimes have to toot our own horns."

"That's true, I did," admitted Mr. Rumpel. "And who knows, maybe she will get a job from all this."

"Can't we go a little faster, Dad?" begged Quincy. "Somebody may be trying to reach me right now."

Quincy sat beside the phone all that afternoon and evening, but the only call that came in was from Grandma, who was wondering how they all were.

The next morning, Quincy was still asleep when the phone rang.

"Quincy! It's for you!" Mrs. Rumpel called up the stairs.

"Me? It's for me?" Rubbing her eyes, Quincy sat upright in bed.

"Yes. Hurry!"

Quincy bolted down the stairs two at a time. "I think it's about a job," whispered her mother, handing her the phone.

Quincy cleared her throat. "Egh, erg-erg, ech. This is me." A long pause, then, "Oh, yes! Absolutely. Oh, lots and lots." Pause. "Oh, really? Sure! I'd love to!" Pause. "Oh, right away. No prob!"

40

Hanging up the phone, she peered at her family, who were standing around waiting to hear the news.

"I got one!" she cried, her eyes wide with wonder. "I GOT A JOB!"

"Exactly where is this job?" her father wanted to know.

"And just who are these people?" asked her mother.

"What will you wear?" wondered Leah.

Morris rubbed his hands together gleefully. "How much? Like, how many loonies do you get?"

Still looking slightly stunned, Quincy said, "Do you know what's unreal? It's practically right next door! Well, at least it's down the road somewhere. That was Mrs. McAddams. I think her husband is a dentist or something. They even know Grandma and Grandpa. Anyway, they have a *big* ranch, and Dr. McAddams is busy doing his dentist stuff, so that's why they need some help."

"You mean you're really going to do ranch work?" asked Leah.

"That's our girl!" Mr. Rumpel put his arm around Quincy's shoulders and gave her a squeeze. "You show 'em, Princess. We Rumpels come from pioneer stock, and ranch work is in our genes."

"Grandpa Twistle worked on a farm in Saskatchewan once," said Mrs. Rumpel.

"Well, it won't be quite *all* ranch work. I'll also be helping out with the kids. I guess I'll be sort of a ranch-nanny."

"A babysitter for the Addams family!" giggled Morris.

Quincy gave him a withering look. "*Mc*Addams, you ninny."

"But you haven't had any nanny training," said Mrs. Rumpel.

"I don't need nanny training. I've had plenty of experience baby-sitting Leah and Morris. Remember that time you and Dad went to the rebounder convention in Victoria?"

"I remember. You and Morris held a rummage sale out in the driveway, and sold off my potted avocado plant and our toaster."

"And they sold all my Barbies. I remember that," said Leah.

"And my collection of old Reader's Digests," grumbled Mr. Rumpel.

"That was ages ago," said Quincy. "Anyway, now I've got a real job and I can start planning for my horse. Oh, and Mrs. McAddams wants me to come over right away."

"I'll drive you there after breakfast," said Mrs. Rumpel.

"But, Mom, nobody gets driven to their job by their *mother*. I can get there by myself."

"No buts. You're not going off to work in some strange place for strange people that we don't know. I'll drive you, and that's that."

9

Dressed in her best jeans and yellow fleece top and with her red hair in a short, skimpy braid, Quincy hurried down to the kitchen. She was just gulping down some cereal when she heard a sloshing sound behind her. It was Morris, staggering in with his aquarium. Leonardo and Donatello were slopping around at the bottom of the seething water.

"I just found it," he gasped, setting the aquarium down on the table. "But my poor little guys must have hated spending last night in the salad bowl. Just look at Leonardo. I think he's brain-damaged. See how his mouth keeps opening and closing? And his eyes aren't twinkly anymore. It's all your fault! Can I go with you to see the Addams family?"

"No, you can't. And their name isn't Addams. Did you buy some fish medicine yesterday?"

Morris shook his head gloomily. "I couldn't find a pet store."

If he just didn't look so dejected and skinny, thought Quincy. *But I'm not going to give in and take him*. "Fish are tough. He'll be all right if you just let him rest for a while."

Just then Mrs. Rumpel flitted through the kitchen with Aunt Ida's rubber plant. "What am I going to do with this?" she cried, holding it out in front of her. "There's no room anywhere."

"Put it out on the porch," said Quincy. "The fresh air will do it good. Can we please go now? The sooner I get there, the sooner I start earning money."

"Where's the sunscreen?" wailed a voice. "I'm coming with you but I can't find the sunscreen. Has anybody seen it?"

Quincy groaned. Leah was standing in the doorway. She was wearing pink shorts over black tights, a long-sleeved T-shirt with a mermaid on it, and her mushroom hat. "Leah, I'm in a hurry! You'll live without sunscreen for a few minutes. Anyway, why do you have to come?"

"To see where you're working. Mom said I could come for the ride."

Morris looked up hopefully. "If you let me come, I could ask Dr. Addams about Leonardo."

"Dr. McAddams is a *dentist*, Morris. Not a fish doctor."

"Or I could just stay here and watch my little guy die . . ."

Quincy knew when she was beaten. "Oh, all right. You can come. But Dr. McAddams has probably left for work by now." *This is really great, isn't it? Arriving at my new job with my entire family in tow . . .*

As they piled into the station wagon, she noticed a figure in a spanking new pair of farmer's overalls standing by the barn, cheerfully waving a straw hat at her.

Quincy waved back. *Thank goodness Dad isn't coming, too,* she thought. Or Snowflake. The big shaggy white dog, his lower half caked in mud, was sitting morosely on the front porch beside the drooping rubber tree plant.

10

"Watch for something saying McAddams," said Quincy, as they pulled out onto the main road.

They drove slowly along, calling out the names on all the mailboxes. Finally they came to a big round white one with a wavy top.

"There it is," said Leah.

Mrs. Rumpel stopped the car. "That's a funny kind of mailbox."

"It's supposed to be a tooth, Mom. A molar. Don't you see that?" Quincy felt her stomach tighten with excitement. *This is it*, she thought. *My very first, real job. And I got it all by myself.*

As they drove down the winding driveway, Leah turned for a last look at the tooth mailbox.

"Something's following us!" she cried.

"A bear!" screeched Morris. "An *Ursus Arctos!*"

Quincy peered over her shoulder at the cloud of dust barrelling along behind them. It was definitely some kind of animal. She could see the legs. *More like a wolf!*

46

"Hit the floorboards, Mom!"

Gripping the steering wheel with both hands, Mrs. Rumpel stepped on the gas. Gradually their pursuer fell behind.

As the car swerved around a bend, a house loomed up in front of them. With two old-fashioned turrets at the corners, it seemed to tower at least three storeys high. Scraggy rose bushes clung to the faded brown shingles and pressed against the windows.

"It looks real spooky," said Morris. "I'll bet they lock up their prisoners in those towers. And I see some bats flying around up there, too."

"They're not bats, they're swallows," said Quincy. "But just look at that. They must have dozens of horses!" And she pointed to a huge old barn, its boards weathered to a dusky silver.

The Rumpels disembarked from the station wagon, and a familiar shape emerged from the dust behind them.

"It's Snowflake," they groaned, as the grimy creature loped joyfully towards them.

Just then a swarm of small, shrieking bodies and balloons spilled out of the house. But when they saw the four Rumpels and Snowflake, there was a sudden silence. Clutching their balloons and seemingly rooted to the spot, the children stood staring solemnly.

"Good grief, Quincy," said Mrs. Rumpel, her voice cracking slightly. "How many are there?"

Quincy did a quick head-count. "I think there are about eleven, Mom. It's hard to tell with all the balloons. Anyway, I can handle eleven."

The cluster of Rumpels advanced, and the screen door banged open again.

"There's more?" gasped Mrs. Rumpel.

But this time only a single figure emerged—full-sized.

"Look," said Quincy, "she's wearing woolly chaps!"

"You must be the Rumpels," called out the wearer of the woolly chaps. "I'm Loralee McAddams. Just call me Loralee."

As they followed her into the house, Quincy paused to wave to the pack of children.

"Hi!" she said, flashing her broadest smile. "I'm your new ranch-nanny. We're going to have packs of fun together!" Smacking their bubblegum, the children stared back at her.

Inside, the Rumpels picked their way through the jumble of sneakers and boots on the floor of the mud room. Quincy sniffed appreciatively. "It smells like a real horse ranch, doesn't it?" she whispered to Leah.

Leah wrinkled her nose. "I think it smells like the boys' gym at school."

In the living-room, their hostess tossed some jackets, toys and cats off the chesterfield and motioned the Rumpels to sit down.

"Sometimes these darn chaps are a pain," she said, seating herself in a rocking chair and attempting to cross her legs.

"I'll bet they're great for riding, though," said Quincy.

"They're supposed to be, but I don't ride. I used to wear them when I was a country and western singer, back on the prairies. Now I just dress up like this for the kids' birthday parties." Reaching up, Mrs. McAddams took off her wide-brimmed western hat, disclosing a tumble of black hair.

"Oh," said Mrs. Rumpel primly. "Then someone must be having a birthday today."

Quincy sank lower into the chesterfield cushions. *Right, Mother.*

"Oh, for sure!" said Mrs. McAddams. "Muggsy. He's turning five already. Would you believe that? Poppy is seven, and Crocus, our little filly, is three."

"That's all? Only three kids?" cried Quincy. *And who knows how many horses! This is going to be a dream job!*

11

"I know your grandma quite well, you know, Quincy," Mrs. McAddams went on. "She used to be in my aerobics class. One of my most energetic pupils, in fact, until she threw her hip out last year in the middle of our Canada Day display."

The screen door banged and the birthday party trooped back in—nine little boys and two girls. The smallest one, with short red hair and new purple overalls, was yelling the loudest.

"My balloon popped and Jason's gum is stuck in his nose and Muggsy has to go to the bathroom but he can't work his zipper and we're hungry. Mommy, when's the birthday cake?"

"It's not ready yet, Crocus," said Loralee, unzipping the zipper and peeling off the gum. "Here's another balloon. How would you all like a carrot muffin?"

There was a murmur of discontent.

"They don't want muffins," said Poppy, who was bigger than the others. "They want cake."

"Not till after lunch." Loralee headed towards the kitchen. "How about some doughnut holes?"

"Yay! Yay!" screeched the mob, following her. "Doughnut holes!"

Mrs. Rumpel's eyes grew misty. "Little Crocus looks just like Quincy used to! The same straight red hair, and the same little overalls. Even the same cute little waddle . . ."

Quincy groaned.

Loralee returned with a mug of coffee for Mrs. Rumpel and a plate of doughnut holes for the others. Then she sat down and proceeded to blow up balloons. "Holes don't seem quite as unhealthy as doughnuts, somehow," she said, between balloons. "Tooth-wise, that is."

Mrs. Rumpel nodded and sipped her coffee. "I can see you're very busy today," she said, when she'd finished. "And we must be on our way." Wiggling her eyebrows at Morris and Leah, she stood up. "We'll pick you up later, Quincy."

"NO! I mean, no thanks, Mom. I'll get home by myself." *Maybe, just maybe, the McAddamses will lend me one of their horses . . .*

It was then that Morris began twitching his nose. "Something sure smells good."

"It's the cake," said Loralee. "Why don't you and your sister stay for the rest of the party? Then you can have some."

51

"Oh, no!" burst out Quincy. "They can't do that! Morris has a sick goldfish at home, and Leah has stuff to do."

"I don't think he's so sick now," said Morris, helping himself to another doughnut hole.

"What stuff?" asked Leah, who seemed to be rooted to the chesterfield.

"You know. All that painting stuff." *I'll just die if they stay. Besides, then Mom would have to pick us all up afterwards and I won't get a chance to ride home on a horse!*

Hauling Leah up from the chesterfield by one arm and giving Morris a pinch on his seat, Mrs. Rumpel propelled the two of them to the door.

"Snowflake," hissed Quincy to her mother. "Take Snowflake, too." But when they looked around outside, he was nowhere to be seen.

As the birthday party gang stood around watching, Mrs. Rumpel shoved Leah and Morris into the car. Then she climbed in herself.

As she watched the old brown station wagon disappear around the bend, Quincy felt a pang of abandonment. But the pang was replaced by a quiver of excitement.

This is finally it, she thought. *The real beginning of my new life.*

Then she felt a poke from behind. She whirled around. Looking up at her from somewhere around her knees was Crocus, her round blue eyes studying Quincy.

52

"What's your name?"

Quincy hesitated. For a moment she was tempted to say Roxy. Then she grinned.

"Quincy," she said. "Quincy Rumpel."

After all, she thought, *my own name has got me through life so far, hasn't it?* Hitching up her jeans, she strode into the house to begin her new duties.

12

Quincy found Mrs. McAddams in the kitchen, mixing up icing.

Loralee pointed to a large dinosaur-shaped cake. "It's a surprise for Muggsy. He loves stegosauruses."

Quincy stared at the cake sitting on a foil-covered cookie sheet. "Oh, but that's not a stegosaurus, Mrs. McAddams," she said. "That's tyrannosaurus rex."

Mrs. McAddams looked at the cake with a worried frown. "Please just call me Loralee," she murmured absently. "Do you think they'll notice?"

"Oh, they'll notice, all right, believe me. I haven't lived all these years with Morris for nothing. But not to worry. I can make it into a stegosaurus. I'll just make his front legs bigger and his head smaller. And I'll trim his tummy to make spikes for his tail and doodads for his back. And then we'll cover him with lots of icing. No one will ever know the difference. Leave everything to me."

Just then the phone rang in the other room. As she dashed away to answer it, Loralee called back, "Go for it, Quincy! There's some food colouring for the icing in the cupboard, and a bag of decorations . . ."

Oh, boy. Now's my chance to really make an impression! thought Quincy. Humming happily to herself, she began to whittle away at the cake with a bread knife. But the pieces she whittled off all crumbled. As the cake shrank, the pile of crumbs grew. Soon there were almost as many crumbs as cake. Tyrannosaurus rex had become an amoeba.

Luckily, Loralee was still talking on the phone. Scooping the crumbs into a bowl, Quincy sprinkled them with warm water. Then she shaped the mixture into the various missing parts and stuck them around what was left of the cake.

Stepping back, she surveyed her creation.

"Oh, no!" she groaned. For it was a dinosaur of no distinguishable shape, and much too small to boot. There was no way it would feed the mob waiting outside.

She looked around frantically. On the counter was a large bag of hotdog buns. Quickly, Quincy made up her mind.

Holding her breath, she sliced the cake in two, separating head from tail. Then she stuffed eight hotdog buns between the sections.

She was just finishing slathering the whole thing with green icing when she heard the sound of creaking leather. It was Loralee in her woolly chaps.

55

"Quincy, you're a marvel!" she cried. "It looks bigger than ever. How did you do it?"

But before Quincy was forced to divulge her secret, the birthday crew came storming in.

* * *

Luckily most of the party-goers preferred their hot-dogs plain, so there was no shortage of buns for lunch.

Then, bravely singing "Happy Birthday, Dear Muggsy," Quincy carried in the cake. There were gasps of delight at the blazing candles and sputter-ing sparklers, and happy shouting over the eleven small rubbery dinosaurs that decorated the top. *All in all, it looks pretty impressive*, thought Quincy.

"Oh, boy! Slime icing!" cried the guests as the cake was set down on the table.

When she cut it, Quincy found the middle some-what tough. But Muggsy and his friends, happily playing with their toy dinosaurs and eating their icing, didn't seem to notice. It was Crocus who made the discovery.

"Hey, there's a bun in my cake!" she cried.

"It's sort of a health cake," mumbled Quincy. "Anyway, it was a stegosaurus, and that's the important thing."

"Stegosaurus? Stegosaurus?" cried Muggsy. "I didn't know it was a stegosaurus! I thought it was a cow!"

13

Back at Rumpel Ranch, Mrs. Rumpel was busy unpacking the sixteen boxes piled on the kitchen floor. Finally, groaning, she sank wearily down onto a chair.

"What's the matter, Mom?" asked Morris, who was sitting at the table polishing his loonies with toothpaste.

"The matter is, I need some help around here."

"But I don't know where all those things go."

"There are other things you could do. I think you should have chores. Leah, too. And just where is she, by the way?"

Morris shrugged. "Outside somewhere, I guess."

"Well, go and find her. I want to talk to you both."

Morris didn't have far to go. Leah was by the barn, braiding Fireweed's mane into numerous tiny stylish braids.

"This is how you do it for horse shows sometimes," she said, as she twisted on another elastic.

"Mom wants to talk to us," said Morris. "And it doesn't look good. Moving sure makes her cranky."

They were ambling back to the house when Leah pointed up the driveway. "Look what's coming!"

"It's sort of a horse!"

Plodding slowly towards them was a small fat pony with something on its back. The pony's stomach swayed rhythmically from side to side. It appeared to have six legs.

As the creature came closer, they saw that two of the appendages belonged to the rider. "It's Quincy on a horse," gasped Leah. "Call Mom and Dad!"

Morris took off. He returned almost immediately with his parents.

Yelling, "Whoa, Zorro!" Quincy swept past her family right up to the porch. There the pony finally stopped in front of the stunted geraniums. When it started to eat what was left of them, Quincy slid stiffly off, rubbing her bottom.

"You were riding bareback!" marvelled Leah.

"I know. I couldn't use the saddle. My behind was too big. And anyway, the stirrups were too short. But, man! Do I love riding! Just trotting along with the wind in my face. How did I look?"

"Sort of like a centipede," said Morris.

"Quince, that wasn't trotting," said Leah.

"He seems like a nice gentle horse," said Mrs. Rumpel. "And you weren't too far off the ground. Is this the one you want to buy?"

58

"Mother, Zorro is Crocus's *pony*! I borrowed it because it's the only one the McAddamses have."

"I thought you said they had a really big ranch," said Mr. Rumpel.

"Oh, they have. They have hundreds of acres. They just don't have any horses yet, except for Zorro. Loralee says Dr. McAddams is working on a special project. When it's done they'll be able to buy scads of horses."

Just then Snowflake trudged into view, tail drooping. He looked dusty and bedraggled.

"Oh, look at poor Snowflake!" cried Leah.

"Poor Snowflake?" exclaimed Quincy. "Ha! He sat on Muggsy's new plastic ball and squashed it. Then he chewed up the bat. He ate a whole bag of cat crumbles and threw up in the mud room. He chased a rabbit under the house and got stuck, and then he went swimming in the dug-out and scared away their ducks!"

* * *

At dinner, sitting on a cushion, Quincy told her family about her day. "Loralee says there's going to be a big sort of fair and auction on Saturday, and we should go because they may have horses for sale! Can we?"

"I don't know," said her mother. "We're pretty busy. I was planning to put new shelf paper in all the kitchen cupboards and drawers on Saturday, so we could unpack the rest of the dishes and things."

"Shelf paper? Oh, man," moaned Quincy. Then she turned to her father. "Loralee says they have lots of farm machinery for sale at the fair, too."

"Farm machinery? Well, I guess we're not *that* busy, are we, Rose?"

"And they have a white-elephant booth where you can buy all kinds of neat stuff," persisted Quincy. "Like, maybe, glass rolling pins and old cuckoo clocks."

"Well, perhaps the shelf paper could wait," said Mrs. Rumpel. "I've been looking for a glass rolling pin and a cuckoo clock for years."

"I wonder what I should wear," said Leah. "Did Loralee say whether people dress up for the fair?"

Quincy shook her head. "We were too busy."

"What did you do all day?" asked her mother.

"Well, you should have seen the birthday cake I made. Actually, I didn't make the *whole* thing. I sort of sculpted it. It was a huge stegosaurus rex. And I covered it with this thick green icing and put little dinosaurs all over the top, between the candles and sparklers."

Morris licked his lips. "I wish I'd had some."

"Well, actually, the middle part had sort of buns in it. You might not have liked it."

"Did you wrangle any cows?" said Leah.

"They haven't got any. They've got this huge old barn, though. It's twice as big as their house. But when I asked Loralee what they kept in there, she

60

just got a funny look on her face and said, 'Our future!' "

"That's weird," said Morris. "I wonder what *is* in there? Did you look?"

Quincy shook her head. "Not yet. I don't think they want me to. It's all shut up tight. But I'm going to find out why. I have a feeling there's something really mysterious going on there!"

14

That night the Rumpels retired early. "Tomorrow's the big day," said Mr. Rumpel. "Our apple trees are coming!"

But Mrs. Rumpel looked worried. "Maybe we shouldn't be planting them in the middle of the summer. Maybe we should have waited till fall."

Mr. Rumpel shook his head. "It would have been nice to wait till we had our post-hole digger, but I always say *the sooner, the better*. We'll water them thoroughly, and they'll do just fine. By the way, where's the camera? We want to be sure and get a picture."

"I hope they come before I leave for work," said Quincy. "I've never seen three hundred apple trees in a bunch before. I bet it will look like a real forest."

As the girls climbed the narrow stairs to their room, they met Morris on his way down. "Where do you think you're going?" asked Quincy.

"I have to get some leaves for my caterpillars. They're getting hungry."

"MOM!" hollered Quincy. "Morris is keeping yucky things in his room again!"

"It's just my little caterpillar guys. They're not going to bother you."

"Morris, put them outside," ordered Mrs. Rumpel. "I told you. You're not to keep dead, smelly things in your room."

"But these aren't dead. They're wiggly and furry, and they don't smell at all. Can't I? Just for tonight? I'll keep their lid on."

When Mrs. Rumpel relented, Quincy and Leah retreated to their room and barricaded themselves in, stuffing some of Quincy's socks under the door, just in case.

After organizing her clothes for the morning and putting her hair up in curlers, Leah climbed into bed. She was asleep almost immediately. Some time later, however, she was awakened by a rustling noise.

"Caterpillars," she cried. "They're coming!"

The light was on. Quincy was sitting cross-legged on the other bed, muttering to herself as she folded and refolded a piece of coloured paper. Suddenly she scrunched it up and hurled it across the room, where it joined a pile of other wads.

"Quince, what are you doing?"

"I'm trying to do an origami frog. But there must be something wrong with this paper. It just won't fold right. Did you know that some people can even do grasshoppers?"

Leah peered at the clock. The alarm was set for six a.m. "It's one o'clock in the morning! Why are you doing this?"

"Because I'm going to teach those kids to do origami today."

"Did Loralee say you had to?"

"Of course not. It's part of my nanny program." Quincy held up a wrinkled piece of green paper. "Does this look like a frog to you?"

Leah shook her head sleepily. "Not much."

Wadding up the paper, Quincy heaved it onto the pile on the floor. "I'm just so mad! I had my week's nanny schedule all planned, and now it's ruined because I need more practice. Do you think I should do kindergym or French lessons tomorrow? Or make macaroni picture frames? I want to do something really special. First impressions are important."

"Didn't you make your first impression today?" mumbled Leah, pulling the quilt up to her chin.

"Heavens, I hope not. Today didn't count. I didn't really get a chance to do much, between the birthday party and Snowflake. I'm going to do all sorts of things with those kids. Maybe we'll do science projects. Do you know any easy science projects? Or, I know. Jig-saw puzzles! We can do jig-saw puzzles one day. And maybe make kites! Those Chinese dragon ones with the long tails. Actually, the more I think about it, the more I think

64

I will do origami tomorrow. That last frog wasn't so bad . . ."

As Quincy babbled on, Leah pulled the covers over her head and rolled the other way. She was trying to decide what she would wear to the fair on Saturday.

15

RIIIIIINNGGG! An arm fluttered out from under the covers and groped about in mid-air. Eventually it collided with the alarm clock on the cluttered night table. There was a sudden silence. Quincy went back to sleep.

The next thing she heard was Morris hollering out in the hall. "The trees are here! The trees are here!"

Quincy glanced at the clock. "Nine! Oh, no!"

Leah was nowhere in sight.

Throwing on some jeans and a tie-dyed sweatshirt, Quincy ran downstairs. The front door was open.

Her father was standing in the driveway, clad in his new straw hat and overalls. His camera hung around his neck. He was waving his arms at a big transport truck backing towards him. Mrs. Rumpel, wearing a bright orange bath towel and a shower cap, hovered by the front door. Leah, in shorts, was perched on the verandah railing swinging her legs, while Morris hopped excitedly from one foot to the other, clutching his jar of caterpillars. He was still in his pyjamas.

The truck stopped, and the driver climbed down. "Rumpel?" he asked.

"Right on!" cried Mr. Rumpel.

"Oh, boy!" shouted Morris. "Here they come!"

Going to the back of the truck, the driver opened the doors and disappeared inside. The Rumpels held their breaths. Finally, the man reappeared with two bundles of bare-looking sticks under his arm, their root-ends wrapped in gunny sacking. The sticks were about a metre long.

"That's it?" gasped Mrs. Rumpel, as he tossed them down onto the ground.

"Oh, there's more," said the driver. "Lots more." And he began heaving the bundles out of the truck.

"I thought they'd be sort of blooming or something," said Leah.

"They're not very big, for all that money," said her mother.

Picking up the bundles, Mr. Rumpel began carrying them towards the house. "Don't forget, these are dwarf trees," he said. "They'll never get *really* big, but the apples will sure be easy to pick. Now, all we have to do is plant them."

"Have to get dressed," muttered Mrs. Rumpel, and with a flash of orange she was gone. She was followed by Leah, who jumped off the railing and darted nimbly into the house behind her. Morris took off around the corner with his caterpillars, while Quincy mumbled "Gotta get to work," and headed for the barn.

Mr. Rumpel watched his family disappear one by one. Then he shrugged and continued carrying his bundles tenderly up onto the verandah.

Half an hour later, when she finally lurched off down the road on Zorro, Quincy was not pleased to see Snowflake slinking along in the ditch behind her.

"Go home! Go home, you crazy dog! I don't want you coming to work with me!" she shouted. But Snowflake, suddenly becoming stone-deaf, trudged on.

As she jiggled up to the front of the McAddams house, Quincy looked around for signs of Dr. McAddams's car, but couldn't see any. *He must have gone already*, she thought. *I'd sure like to see what he looks like!*

After rubbing down Zorro and turning him out to graze, she went inside. Loralee was rushing around in her nightgown, getting ready to go to town. Poppy was working on a computer in the corner of the living-room, and Crocus was sticking cheese slices on the window. All the while, Muggsy roared up and down the hall on his new black plastic birthday motorcycle.

"Come on, you guys!" cried Quincy. "I've got some real fun stuff to do. Have you got some coloured paper? Come here and I'll show you something really neat.''

"I'm already doing fun stuff," said Crocus, plastering another cheese slice on the window.

"So am I," yelled Muggsy, careening past.

"But this is even more fun," shouted Quincy, leaping out of the way. "We're going to make little paper frogs.''

Poppy looked up from her computer. "Do you mean origami? We already did that in school. I made a grasshopper. Now I'm writing a novel about a dog who goes to the moon in a lunar module. I'm on Chapter 18.''

"Oh."

As she looked out through the window, Quincy noticed Snowflake peering wistfully in between the cheese slices. Slowly, an idea began to come to her.

It was her greatest idea yet. And one that could make money to buy her horse, to boot.

16

"All right, mes enfants, I want everyone outside. Tout de suite, s'il vous plaît!"

Poppy looked up at Quincy. "Pourquoi?" she sighed.

"Wheeeeee!" hollered Muggsy, pedalling furiously past, this time with Crocus hanging on behind.

Quincy groaned.

Just then, Loralee's bedroom door was flung open and she popped out, wearing green tights and a star-spangled exercise suit. Darting from child to child, she kissed them.

"I'm late for my class. Can you handle things, Quincy?"

"Oh, you bet, Loralee."

"For lunch, Poppy likes a grilled orange cheese sandwich, on white, with a pickle. Muggsy likes white cheese and peanut butter on brown, no marg, and *don't cut it*, whatever you do. No pickle. Crocus sometimes has a plain orange cheese slice on brown, cut in four, crusts off, and just a little may-

70

onnaise, and a pickle. If she won't eat that, you could try a hard-boiled egg, but take out the yolk . . .''

"Sure, don't worry. I'll feed her something.''

"Emergency numbers by the phone and Band-aids in bathroom . . .'' Loralee's voice trailed off as she went out the door.

As Mrs. McAddams climbed into the pickup, Quincy hollered, "Is it all right if we make something?''

Loralee waved her arm out the window and clattered off down the driveway.

I guess that means it's okay, thought Quincy. With Snowflake trudging along beside them, she steered her charges towards the barn.

"We're not supposed to play in there,'' said Poppy.

"Oh? Well, we won't play. I just want to look for some wood, because we're going to do something special today. We are going to make a dog cart. Then you can all go for rides. Won't that be fun?''

"Oh, boy!'' said Muggsy. Then he frowned. "But we haven't got a dog . . .''

"*We* have Snowflake. Samoyeds like him pull big sleds up in the North. They *love* to pull things.'' Quincy's eyes sparkled as she thought of future possibilities. *People would probably pay good money to go for a dog-cart ride. People like the ones going to the fair on Saturday.*

"I'm sure we can find some boards in the barn
. . ."

The heavy barn door creaked as she pulled it open
and stepped inside. The cool darkness closed
around her, and she realized she was alone. The
three little McAddamses were clustered outside,
staring in.

As her eyes became accustomed to the dimness,
Quincy could make out the cattle stanchions and old
feeding troughs in the middle of the barn. Against
the outer wall were box stalls for horses. They were
all empty. The dirt floor was packed hard from
ancient use. Pervading everything was the faint
smell of hay, old rope and leather, and animals.
Except for the buzzing of flies, it was deathly quiet.

It's eerie in here, she thought. Then, as she looked
around, she noticed the walled-off room in one corner. The heavy plank door was bolted shut and
locked with a padlock.

17

Quincy heard a rustle behind her. It was Poppy, Muggsy and Crocus scuffing through the old straw that covered the floor of the barn.

"I guess it's all right to come in if you're with us," said Poppy.

Quincy pointed to the locked door. "What's in there?"

"Daddy's stuff," said Muggsy.

"His teeth," said Crocus.

"His *what*?"

"His *teeth*," repeated Poppy. "And something else. Something that's a *secret*."

"Why aren't you allowed to play in here?"

"Because it's *dangerous*!" said Crocus.

Quincy looked around nervously. *Oh, wow*, she thought. *This is pretty weird stuff. We'd better get out of here in a hurry*. But she couldn't resist asking, "Why does your dad keep his teeth locked up in that room?"

"He's saving them," said Muggsy.

Suddenly Quincy had a vision of the as yet unknown, and apparently toothless, dentist — counting and re-counting his molars and bicuspids behind the locked door. *But what was the secret?* She would get to the bottom of it sooner or later, but first she had a dogcart to build.

"Hokay! Well, then, let's find those boards and get out of here! And we'll need some nails and a hammer and probably a saw. Oh, yes, and some wheels . . . maybe from an old tricycle or something?"

"I know where all that stuff is," said Muggsy, and he scurried off. Quincy breathed a sigh of relief when they finally emerged with their equipment into the bright sunshine.

"I'll do the hammering and sawing," said Quincy. "You can all be my helpers and hand me stuff."

But this system didn't work for long. Nails were dropped, to be lost forever in the grass. Helpers wandered away. The hammer disappeared mysteriously, and reappeared again.

"This is boring," said Crocus after a while. "I'm hungry."

"You're doing all the fun part," complained Poppy. "And I'm hungry, too. Aren't you going to give us any lunch?"

"I wanna saw something," cried Muggsy. "I'm tired of being a helper."

Finally Quincy laid down her tools. "Okay, we'll break for lunch. But we haven't got much time, you know. We want to finish this today."

So they all filed back into the house. While her charges washed up, Quincy began making sandwiches.

Let's see now, was that white grilled cheese on brown and orange cheese on white . . .

* * *

After lunch the little McAddamses went outside. Quincy cleaned up the kitchen and headed for the bathroom. Then, as she closed the door, she saw them. White and woolly, with leather straps. Loralee's sheepskin chaps! Just hanging there from a hook on the back of the door.

Forgetting what she'd come in for, Quincy fastened them on. Standing on Crocus's little sink stool, she pirouetted in front of the bathroom mirror. The leather made just the slightest of slight creaking noises.

Oh, wow! They're perfect!

The front door banged. Quincy was frantically unbuckling the chaps when someone pounded on the bathroom door.

"Quincy, I used up all the nails and now the cart's all done!" hollered Muggsy through the keyhole. "Are you coming out soon?"

Outside Quincy hammered down the pointy ends of the nails and set the cart on two old tricycle wheels. Then it was given a quick coat of Poppy's blue poster paint.

"It's beautiful!" said Poppy. "Let's put on some Christmas bells, too."

"And some balloons!" cried Crocus.

"It needs a honker," said Muggsy, and he brought out the horn from his motorcycle. Then they added some velvet cushions (in case of slivers) and an umbrella (because of the hole in the ozone).

The engineers were overwhelmed with their handiwork. "It's sort of like Cinderella's coach," said Poppy. "Can I go first? I'm the oldest."

"I should be first," argued Muggsy. "I did most of the hammering."

"Me!" squealed Crocus. "I wanna be Cinderella!"

As this would be Snowflake's debut as a sled-dog, Quincy decided he should start out with the lightest load available — Crocus.

18

This has got to work, Quincy told herself. *I'll never make a fortune just being a nanny. I know* that. *So if I want a horse this summer, I have to find the money some other way. And giving dog-cart rides at the fair could be the way! I'll get Morris to collect the money and I'll do the rest . . .*

She looked at Snowflake sleeping peacefully in the sun. *He'll look great pulling the cart on Saturday. I just hope he remembers to curl up his tail like he's supposed to.*

Nudging the dog awake, Quincy coaxed him over to the cart and put the rope harness around him. ''I'd better lead him. He's not very used to doing this.''

''But I wanna do it myself,'' said Crocus, seating herself on a cushion and opening the umbrella.

''Not this time,'' said Quincy. Taking hold of the reins, she stood beside Snowflake, who had sat down to scratch himself.

''All right, let's go! MUSH! MUSH! Please, Snowflake. Go! Giddyup!''

Snowflake gazed at Quincy with puzzled brown eyes, but his rear end remained solidly planted on the ground.

"I wanna go!" hollered Crocus, bobbing her umbrella up and down.

Just then a rabbit scampered around the end of the barn. Snowflake sprang into action. Yelping excitedly, he bolted across the barnyard with Crocus and the cart rattling along behind. Also loping along behind came Quincy, hanging onto the reins for dear life.

That's when total disaster struck.

First came a splintering sound. The two wheels fell off and rolled away into the grass. For a fleeting instant, just before the rope was jerked out of her hands and she toppled over backwards, Quincy caught a glimpse of something purple sailing through the air.

She scrambled to her feet just in time to glimpse Snowflake disappearing behind the barn, still dragging the disintegrating cart. Balloons, cushions and pieces of blue boards were everywhere.

Then from the sandbox under the poplar tree came a howl of indignation.

Quincy stumbled over and found Crocus sitting in a little heap in the middle of a squashed sandcastle.

"Are you all right?" she cried. "Do your bones feel all right and everything?"

"Blechht!" Crocus spat out some sand. Her face crumpled. "My leg feels funny, Quincy. It hurts."

"Maybe she broke her femur," said Poppy, running over. Crocus's sobs turned to bellows.

Quincy knelt down and put her arms around her. Lifting the little purple pant-leg, she peeked at Crocus's small brown leg. It seemed normal. Or did it?

What was it Gwen used to say? Her cousin Gwen, who was always showing off about her first-aid course. Suddenly Quincy remembered. *Don't move the patient if a fracture is suspected*. Unless, of course you were in the middle of a fire, or something . . .

"Crocus, stay still and don't move. I'm going into the house to phone somebody. You kids stay here and watch her. Don't let her stand up or anything."

"I wanna popsicle," sobbed Crocus. "A purple one."

"You've got it!" cried Quincy as she sprinted towards the house.

By the time she reached the phone she was shaking all over. At first she could hardly focus on the numbers posted on the wall. Finally she got through to Dr. McAddams's office.

"Do you wish to make an appointment?" asked someone.

"No! No! This is an emergency! I have to talk to Dr. McAddams!"

"Have you lost a filling?"

"No! This is his ranch-nanny. It's about Crocus!"

79

In a moment a low voice came on. "Yes? What is it?"

His voice sounds hollow, thought Quincy. *Maybe it's because of his teeth*. "This is Quincy Rumpel, sir. It's Crocus. She looks all right but maybe she isn't. You see, she wanted to be Cinderella in the dog cart. But Snowflake bolted — the darn mutt — and she sort of fell out and landed in the sandbox. I'm not letting her move, in case her leg is broken or something, and I'm going to take a first-aid course like Gwen as soon as I can, but what should I do now?"

"I'm in the middle of a root canal and can't come right away myself, but I'll send out the ambulance. She's not unconscious, is she?"

"Oh, no, sir. She's hollering like anything. And she wants a popsicle."

"Just keep her still and don't let her catch a chill. I'll be there as quickly as I can. I'll get the full story from you then."

Hoo, boy. I'm in for it now, thought Quincy, as she hung up the phone.

When the ambulance came, the attendants found their patient in the sandbox, wrapped up in several woollen blankets and sucking her third popsicle. Broken blue boards were scattered around and an umbrella hung upside down in a nearby tree. Sitting forlornly under a lilac bush was a big white dog with bells looped around his neck.

19

When Dr. McAddams and Loralee arrived home, they found Crocus in a reclining lawn chair padded with pillows. Stuffed animals had been tucked in all around her. While Poppy and Muggsy ran back and forth to the house bringing her various treats and toys, Crocus sat happily eating doughnut holes and the last piece of birthday cake.

As Loralee wrote out a cheque for the ambulance, Dr. McAddams strode over to Quincy, who was untangling balloons from the tree.

Quincy watched him warily. He was dressed in grey slacks and a Mickey Mouse sweatshirt. His medical mask still dangled around his neck. A cowlick of hair like Morris's waved in the breeze as he advanced, and his blue eyes looked worried.

"Where did you get all this stuff to make a cart?" he asked, surveying the scattered blue boards.

Quincy gulped. "In the barn, sir. They were just some old boards Muggsy found. I didn't think you'd mind."

"I don't mind about the boards. I mind that you might have had a much more serious accident. And I mind that the kids went in the barn when they knew they weren't supposed to."

Oh, man! I'm going to lose my job for sure! Quincy couldn't think of what to say. Finally she blurted out, "I'm sorry, sir. It's my fault. I told them to. But it won't happen again, I promise!" *His voice is so different than it was on the phone. Not hollow at all . . .*

"That's good," said Dr. McAddams. Then, looking at the disconsolate Snowflake, he added, "And perhaps in the future it would be better if you left your dog at home."

"Oh, I will, sir. I guarantee it!"

* * *

Back at Rumpel Ranch, the rest of the Rumpels were eating their stir-fry tofu dinner when Morris cried, "I hear a siren!"

Mr. and Mrs. Rumpel stared at one another. Then, pushing back their chairs, they jumped up and rushed outside after Morris and Leah.

An ambulance was pulling up in front of the house. As the Rumpels watched open-mouthed, the back doors swung open, and Snowflake jumped out. He was followed by Quincy.

"Thanks a lot, guys!" she called to the attendants, who waved cheerily back as they took off up the driveway.

82

Quincy walked into the house, stretching and yawning. "Boy, am I tired."

"Who's in the ambulance?" cried Mrs. Rumpel.

"Nobody. Well, nobody besides those two guys. What's for supper?"

"Can you hear the siren when you're inside?" asked Morris.

"Sort of. Actually, they only turned it on because I asked them to when we got here. Crocus didn't need it after all. Her ankle is just *strained*, you see. That's not as serious as *sprained*. Dr. McAddams and Loralee came home early after I phoned him about the accident, so Veronica and Bill gave me a lift here in the ambulance. They're really cool. I'm going to take a first-aid course real soon. But I don't know whose teeth are locked up in the barn. They sure don't seem to belong to Dr. McAddams. It's too bad I won't be able to sell dog-cart rides at the fair on Saturday. The cart is all smashed up, thanks to flaky Snowflake. So now I'm back to square one."

In stunned silence, the Rumpels listened to this breathless summary of Quincy's day. Finally, her mother spoke. "Square one? You mean you lost your job already?"

"Oh, no. Not quite. But after today, I don't think the McAddamses are going to give me a raise or anything. And it will take forever to save up enough for a horse on my salary. So I'm desperate to raise some cash. Have you got any ideas, Morris?"

Morris pursed his lips thoughtfully. "I'll pay you big bucks if you plant my share of the apple trees."

"You mean they aren't all planted yet?"

"Are you kidding?" said Leah. "And it's been horrible. Like a slave camp. Look, I've even got a callus."

"I wouldn't mind planting trees," said Quincy. "Strictly for financial reasons. But I've still got my daytime job, you know."

"You could plant the trees at night," said Morris. "I'll rent you my big flashlight."

For a moment Quincy considered the proposal. "How much will you pay me?"

"A nickel a tree. And I'll let you use my flashlight all night for a loonie."

"Forget it, buster!"

20

The weary tree planters were still asleep the next morning when Quincy strapped on her backpack and set off on her bike. She was followed, as usual, by the determined Snowflake, slinking along unseen in the ditch behind her.

But when Quincy got to the McAddams farmhouse, she was surprised to see the dentist's big black car in the driveway.

This is odd. He's usually gone by the time I get here. Is Crocus's ankle worse?

Dropping her bike, she hurried towards the house.

Suddenly the door burst open. Quincy breathed a sigh of relief as Crocus ran out to meet her. Her purple overalls were on backwards and her eyes were wide with alarm, but at least her ankle seemed all right.

"What's wrong?" asked Quincy.

"Daddy's teeth are gone!"

Here we go again! Those teeth! What's with them, anyway?

At the front door, she was met by Poppy and Muggsy. "Somebody stole . . ." began Muggsy breathlessly.

"Your dad's teeth. I know."

"Yes, and we're looking for them," said Poppy, as they darted away.

Dr. McAddams was sitting at the kitchen table, his head in his hands. Loralee, her hair hanging limply over her pale face and her dragon-embroidered kimono hanging sashless, was making a pot of coffee.

"I'm sorry about your teeth," said Quincy. She didn't know what else to say.

Dr. McAddams looked up with bloodshot eyes. "Thank you."

"There were ninety-three, you know," said Loralee. "He was going to start testing when he got a hundred, and now they're gone. All gone."

"Ninety-three *teeth*?"

"Ninety-three. And these weren't just your ordinary run-of-the-mill teeth, either. These were baby central incisors. It took us years to collect them. Remember when we found the first one in that cow pasture on our honeymoon, Orville?"

Quincy gulped. "A baby's tooth in a *cow pasture*?"

"They can be anywhere, you know. We found one in the back of a horse trailer."

Quincy felt a shiver run down her spine. *This is even weirder than I thought.*

86

"Usually, though, they just fall out into the grass or get lost in the hay, and then nobody finds them," said Dr. McAddams. "It's not as if horses put them under their pillows for the tooth fairy, you know."

"Tooth fairy? Horses?" Quincy sank weakly down onto a chair. "You mean you were just collecting *horse* teeth?"

"Not *just*, Quincy. Baby horse teeth are hard to come by. And Orville has to have them if he's going to do his project."

"We may as well tell her everything, now that it's all over. You see . . ." But Dr. McAddams seemed unable to go on.

"You see," continued Loralee, sitting down across the table from Quincy, "Orville had an idea for a special Canadian breed of horse — one with super-good teeth. So he's been developing various plastic coatings. But they have to be tested on baby horse teeth that are still in good condition. And now they're all gone."

"I didn't know horses even had baby teeth."

"Of course they do," said Dr. McAddams, perking up a little. "All mammals do. Horses usually get their first one at ten days, and they have six teeth at a year. By the time they're three, two or three teeth will have already been replaced. And by the time they're five, all their baby teeth have been replaced. So there must be lots of horse teeth lying around somewhere. It's just that it's so hard to find them. Practically impossible."

87

All at once Quincy felt her old investigative powers returning. "I presume you've searched the premises?"

"Of course." Dr. McAddams sounded a little impatient. "We've been looking since daybreak."

"Oh. Have you considered espionage? Maybe there are international implications." Quincy didn't quite know where these words were coming from, but they seemed to suit the occasion. "I mean, because of the *Canadian* part?"

"I doubt that, Quincy."

"Oh. But it *could* be. Anyway, how did someone get into the room? I saw a big padlock on the door."

"There is. And it's still there."

"Aha. Is there a window?"

"A really small one," said Loralee. "High up."

"H'mmmm. And was it open or shut?"

"I always leave it a little open," said Dr. McAddams. "But hooked on the inside. And now it's unhooked and wide open." He shook his head in bewilderment.

"Aha. H'mmmm. Obviously an outside job. Oh, and were the teeth *in* anything? I mean, like a bottle or something?"

"Not a bottle," said Loralee. "My red suede purse with the zipper and the gold chain handle."

"H'mmmm. I think I'll check things out, if that's all right."

The McAddamses nodded glumly.

Hitching up her jeans, Quincy strode out of the house. Obviously, this case was going to take priority over her nanny work today!

Quincy Rumpel, Private Investigator, felt the adrenalin surge through her veins (arteries?). It was going to be tough, but she would crack this case. She would find the missing teeth and save the McAddams Project from going down the drain!

21

For a moment Quincy found herself thinking of Freddie. They had made a good team when they solved the Brass Monkey Case. Well, Freddie was ancient history now. She was on her own.

At the barn, she seemed to bump into little McAddamses everywhere she turned. They were swinging from doors, climbing ladders, jumping down from the hay loft . . .

"I thought you weren't supposed to be in here," said Quincy.

"We're looking for Daddy's teeth!" shouted Muggsy, swinging down from the roof on a rope.

Quincy was strolling around looking for clues when Poppy suddenly jumped down from the hay-loft. Muggsy disengaged himself from the rope, and Crocus scrambled out of a manger. As all three lined up behind her, Quincy turned and saw Dr. McAddams's silhouette framed in the open door of the barn.

"Oh, sir," she said, "we were just looking around for clues."

Dr. McAddams grunted. Taking a key out of his pocket, he headed across the shadowy barn, followed by Quincy and the three children.

"It would sure help if I could see the actual site of the crime," she said hopefully.

Dr. McAddams grunted again. Unlocking the padlock, he opened the door of the locked room.

Quincy quickly inspected it. The walls, floor and ceiling were made of rough planks. A single square window, no larger than a computer screen, swung gently back and forth on the morning breeze. On a shelf above a work table stood dozens and dozens of neatly labelled bottles. Scattered all over the table were pencils, measuring spoons and paper clips.

Dr. McAddams pointed to the labelled bottles on the shelf. "Chemicals for my experiments—resins and plastics for the special coatings. That's why the room was kept padlocked."

"And you were almost ready to start testing them," commiserated Quincy. "And then the McAddams Project would be on the way. On the way to make Canada famous with super-teeth horses. What rotten luck. What a dirty trick!"

She scratched her head thoughtfully. "Were any of your paper clips stolen?"

"I don't know," said Dr. McAddams. "Who counts paper clips?"

This has got to be the most baffling case I've ever been on, thought Quincy.

Just then she heard a small, peevish voice behind her. "We're hungry, Quincy. Will you take us on a Teddy Bears' Picnic?"

Quincy had forgotten all about Poppy, Muggsy and Crocus. "A Teddy Bears' Picnic? Gee, I don't . . . Well, sure, Crocus. Why not?" *If I can't find Dr. McAddams's missing teeth, maybe I can show him what a good ranch-nanny I am . . .*

As she followed the little McAddamses out, Quincy looked back at Dr. McAddams. He was counting his paper clips.

* * *

Carting a picnic basket full of assorted cheese sandwiches, a hard-boiled egg and a thermos of juice, Quincy led Poppy, Muggsy and Crocus along a shady path into some nearby woods.

Behind Quincy came Poppy, wearing sunglasses and carrying a hand compass. She had three teddy bears and a Jungle Barbie in her backpack. Muggsy rode his plastic motorcycle, with a scruffy one-legged, eyeless teddy tucked under his arm. Crocus's bears were both dressed in purple scarves.

It's really peaceful here in the woods, thought Quincy, as the little procession trudged along. *It's so quiet. Just those birds twittering . . .*

Suddenly the silence was broken by a blood-curdling yell from Crocus. Then Muggsy hollered, as his plastic motorcycle was rear-ended. Poppy began to shriek. Quincy stumbled as something hurled itself against the back of her legs.

Knocked down onto her hands and knees, Quincy looked up. A white blur was barrelling down the trail ahead, yipping.

"You darn dog!" yelled Quincy. "What are you doing here?"

Nose to the ground, Snowflake doubled back over his tracks, then stopped at the bottom of an old cottonwood tree. He stood staring up into its branches, whining.

As Quincy scrambled to her feet, she noticed something shiny lying on the ground in front of her.

Paper clips. A little heap of them, almost hidden in the dead leaves.

Peering down from a fork in the old tree were three small masked faces. And dangling from a branch beside them was a red suede purse with a gold chain.

22

"Raccoons?" cried Loralee. "Those cute little animals with the black masks?"

"And the clever little fingers," added Dr. McAddams, happily spreading out his teeth on the kitchen table.

"I guess all they really wanted was the gold chain," marvelled Quincy. "And some paper clips."

"They were smart to unhook that window like they did," said Poppy. "But not quite smart enough to undo the zipper."

"Zippers are pretty hard," said Muggsy.

Setting her two teddy bears on the table, Crocus began rewrapping them in their scarves. "I think Snowflake was the smartest."

"You're absolutely right, honey," said Dr. McAddams. "Snowflake is the real hero of the day. We would never have found the purse without him."

Poppy looked at her father severely through her sunglasses. "Aren't you sorry you called him a bird-brained elephant yesterday, Daddy?"

"Your father was just upset about the cart accident," said Loralee. "He didn't mean it."

"Yes, I'm sorry," said Dr. McAddams, putting his teeth away in a clean mayonnaise jar. "And we're going to make it up. I think Quincy and Snowflake deserve a reward!"

* * *

Quincy declined an invitation to join the McAddamses in a celebration dinner in town. Instead, she pedalled off home in a state of great excitement. In her pocket was an envelope containing cash (!!!) and on her legs (as an extra thank-you from Loralee) were the woolly chaps.

23

Huffing and puffing, Quincy pedalled laboriously homeward in her woolly chaps. She was thinking about the next day. The day of the fair. And maybe, just maybe, the day of her horse!

It was late that afternoon when she finally skidded to a stop in front of Rumpel Ranch. She was surprised to see her parents and Leah sprawled out on kitchen chairs on the verandah, while Morris lay limply on the grass, surrounded by chickens. Everybody looked muddy.

Waving her envelope, Quincy creaked up the steps. "Look, everybody! Loralee gave me her woolly chaps! And guess what? Some raccoons heisted Dr. McAddams's teeth and Snowflake found them, and I got a reward *and* I got paid already. Ta-da! They also invited Snowflake and me to have dinner with them to celebrate, but I wanted to get home and count my money. What have you guys been doing all day? Is the tree planting all finished?"

Mr. Rumpel pointed towards two scraggly rows of brown sticks in one corner of the orchard.

"*We're* all finished!" moaned Leah.

"I'm dead meat!" groaned Morris.

"Your father is going to look for a post-hole digger at the fair tomorrow," said Mrs. Rumpel, brushing chunks of mud from her knees. "And then he can plant the rest of the trees by himself."

Grinning broadly, Mr. Rumpel pulled his straw hat down over his eyes and went to sleep.

* * *

The Rumpels were just finishing the dishes when Snowflake arrived. After enjoying dinner at McDonald's with the McAddamses, he had been driven home in their big black car. "He ate three Big Macs and a bunch of chicken nuggets," reported Muggsy. "Then he had some fries and a chocolate sundae."

* * *

The next morning Quincy was the first one awake. For a few minutes she lay in bed counting and recounting her money. Loralee had generously paid her for a full week, even though she had only worked three days ($80). She added to that her reward money ($100), an advance on several weeks' allowance ($20), an advance on her next year's birthday money ($25), and a small demand loan from Morris ($10).

"Leah! Wake up! Guess how much money I've got? Two hundred and thirty-five dollars. Cash! I bet that's enough to buy a pretty good horse at the auction today, huh?"

"Whadja say?"

Quincy flapped the money over Leah's head. "I said I've got *two hundred and thirty-five dollars!*"

"Well, you'd better stop waving it around. You're going to lose it."

"Don't worry. It's going right into my fanny-pack."

Wadding her money into the pouch, Quincy strapped it around her waist. Then she inspected herself in the mirror.

This is what I looked like the day I bought my horse, she said to herself. A thin braid of red hair brushed the shoulder of her plaid cotton shirt. Her new jeans were baggy, but that was because her mother had bought them. Anyway, they were partly covered up by her woolly chaps. Too bad about her sneakers, but someday she would have real western boots, and a cowboy hat, too.

These chaps are going to take a little getting used to, she thought as she made her way cautiously down the stairs.

She walked stiff-legged into the kitchen, where Morris was stuffing a pancake into his mouth. "Ha, ha!'' he chortled, spraying crumbs. ''You walk like a duck!''

Just then Leah appeared wearing a pink sweater and shorts over black tights. She was carrying her painting of *The Last Dandelions*. ''Grandma phoned yesterday and she thinks I should take my picture to the fair. She thinks it's really good.''

''Holy cow!'' cried Morris suddenly. ''Look at Mom and Dad!''

Mr. and Mrs. Rumpel, dressed for their first public appearance in Cranberry Corners, entered the kitchen together. They wore matching western-style shirts with red roses embroidered on the front. Mr. Rumpel had on stiff new jeans from Workworld. Mrs. Rumpel wore a long, full, blue denim skirt with a white ruffle around the bottom. They both had on new white cowboy hats.

''Look what we've got for you!'' they cried, and they whipped three more hats out from behind their backs.

24

In the rear of the station wagon, beside Leah's picture, Quincy put Grandma's old saddle and bridle—just in case. Then, her heart thumping with excitement and her fanny-pack firmly in place on her stomach (where she could see it), she manoeuvred herself into the back seat between Leah and Morris.

Leaving Snowflake at home sleeping off last night's dinner, the Rumpels set off in their new hats. They had no sooner pulled onto the main road, however, when Leah complained, "The wool from your chaps is sticking all over my tights." She squirmed away from her sister.

Quincy shifted the other way and tried to cross her legs, but it was hopeless. "Ouch. Look out. You kicked me!" complained Morris. "Gee whiz. It's like sitting beside the Lone Ranger. All you need is a mask."

"That's it!" cried Quincy. "That's why Dr. McAddams's voice was so funny on the phone the other day. He had his dentist mask on!"

The fair was swarming with people. The Rumpels parked on the grass between a cattle truck and a horse trailer.

"A horse trailer!" yelped Quincy, leaping out of the car. "I knew there'd be horses here!"

Mr. Rumpel sniffed the air. "Just smell those diesel fumes," he sighed, and promptly headed for the farm machinery.

"I smell food," said Morris, and he took off in another direction.

"Meet back here for lunch!" hollered Mrs. Rumpel.

Leah, clutching *The Last Dandelions*, was feeling nervous, so her mother said she would go with her to find the art show.

"I'm going to look for horses," said Quincy. Putting on her hat, she set off with a rolling gait towards a likely looking building.

It turned out to contain various crafts. Also rabbits, chickens, guinea pigs, kittens and goats — all for sale. The next building smelled better. It had only a display of gigantic vegetables and home-cooking. Moseying along among the cakes, pies, cookies and zucchini loaves was Morris.

"Morris!" shouted Quincy, pushing her way through the crowd. "Have you seen the horses?"

The white hat nodded up and down. "They're out behind. I want my ten dollars back now."

"But you lent it to me and I'm paying good interest."

"It's a demand loan, and I'm demanding it back now. I want to buy that chocolate cake with the Smarties on top." Morris pointed to the biggest cake on the table.

"Well, you can't have your money. I may need it for my horse." Turning around, Quincy struggled back through the crowd to the door.

Outside, she found a little cluster of people following the auctioneer towards a paddock. She hustled over and joined them.

There were six horses. Four were huge—dapple greys with black stockings. Percherons, she heard someone say. Beautiful, but bigger than she had in mind.

Then there was the quarterhorse. Sleek and muscular, with a gleaming chestnut coat and mane, and a white blaze. Nostrils flaring, it galloped back and forth, giving little bucks and kicking up its heels.

Oh, I love you! thought Quincy. *You're exactly what I want. I could ride you to the ends of the earth!*

She could barely see the last horse. It stood alone in the farthest corner, its head hanging down dejectedly. It was pale sandy yellow in colour, with a dark, ragged mane and tail, and so thin its ribs showed.

As Quincy leaned against the rail, the girl standing beside her turned around. "It's too bad about that little buckskin," she said. "She was a range pony, and she's really sound. But after she was brought in, she just began to pine away."

102

Quincy shoved back her hat so she could see better. "Gee, that's really sad. Do you know all about these horses?"

"Most of them. I came to check out the quarter-horse. He's nice, but he's not registered, so the stable I work for isn't interested. He'll probably go for a reasonable price, too, because he's quite green."

Quincy tried to look knowledgeable. "Really?" she croaked.

The girl nodded. "He'd need some breaking in, of course. Lunging, and so forth."

"Oh, of course!"

"Why don't you bid on him? Most of the people here are only interested in the heavy horses."

My dreams are coming true! thought Quincy. *Oh, please, don't let anyone else want him!*

As two men entered the paddock and led the Percherons out two by two, the auctioneer began to shout. He rattled off most of the words so fast that Quincy couldn't understand any of them. It seemed that quite a few people wanted the big horses, because the numbers kept getting higher and higher.

Quincy's head was spinning. Finally she whispered to the girl, "Are they talking about *hundreds* of dollars?"

"Thousands."

It was over in a few minutes. The Percherons were led away, and most of the people wandered off.

103

Next the buckskin mare was led out.

"Who'll start the bidding on this little beauty?" asked the auctioneer. There was scattered laughter.

One man, rolling a cigarette as he slouched against the rail, called out, "Fifty."

"I'm bid fifty dollars." The auctioneer sounded bored. "How about seventy-five?" The man shook his head.

"But I think he wants her," said Quincy.

"Oh, he wants her all right," laughed the girl. "Everybody knows who he is. He buys unwanted horses and ships them off for dog food."

"Going for fifty, folks. Do I hear another bid? GOING . . . GOING . . ."

Suddenly a voice yelled, "Two hundred and thirty-five!"

Everybody looked at Quincy, and she realized the voice had been her own.

"SOLD! To the young lady in the big white hat, for two hundred and thirty-five dollars!"

The man with the cigarette stuck it in his mouth and walked away in disgust.

While Quincy's head whirled, somebody thrust a piece of paper at her and took her money. "My horse!" she cried. "Where's my horse?"

"Right here, cowboy. She's all yours."

Quincy felt a rope being put into her hand. At the other end of it was the buckskin mare, eyeing her with apprehension.

"Oh, baby, it's all right!" cried Quincy. "You're safe now!"

Then, leading her horse, she went to find her family.

25

Quincy found her mother sitting on a blanket in front of the car, reading a book. It was called *How to Make Dining Room Furniture From Plastic Pipes*.

Mom must have found the white-elephant stall, she thought.

"Where is everybody?"

"Leah is at the art display in the chicken shed. Morris borrowed some money. He wants to buy something, I guess. And I haven't seen your father since we got here. Oh, look out, dear. There's a horse behind you!"

"It's all right, Mom. It's my new horse. I just bought her."

"Are you sure she's not too wild? She doesn't look as quiet as that one you rode home the other day . . ."

"She's not too wild, Mom."

At that moment Leah appeared. "I sold it!" she cried. "I sold *The Last Dandelions* for five dollars." Then she saw Quincy's horse.

"You got a buckskin!"

"Yes. Isn't she absolutely gorgeous? I think I'll call her Roxy."

"Excuse me! Excuse me!" The shrill little voice sounded familiar. Then Morris staggered through the crowd carrying the chocolate cake and an old wooden tub.

"It's a butter churn, almost," he gasped, setting his purchases down on the blanket. "Just part of it's missing. I might go into the butter business someday if we get a cow. Hey! You got a yellow one!"

"It's called buckskin, and her name is Roxy."

Finally Mr. Rumpel arrived, carrying a bag of hot dogs, drinks, doughnuts and ice cream bars. He was grinning broadly.

"You look too happy," said Mrs. Rumpel. "What else did you buy, Harvey?"

"Just the post-hole digger. Oh, yes," — Mr. Rumpel's voice faded to a mumble — "and a little green tractor." Then he quickly turned to Quincy. "Say, that's a mighty fine hoss you've got there, podner!"

"Thanks, Dad." Quincy flicked some of Morris's fried onions off her woolly chaps. Then, while her horse grazed contentedly on a patch of green grass beside the blanket, she began to tidy the tangled black mane with her hairbrush.

Life just can't get any better than this, Quincy Rumpel! she thought.

Collect the Quincy Rumpel series!

Quincy Rumpel

Quincy Rumpel wants pierced ears, curly hair and a Save-the-Whales T-shirt.

Her sister, Leah, can't see why she shouldn't have pierced ears, too, while Morris, her brother, longs for a dog.

Mrs. Rumpel hopes for rain, so her job at the umbrella shop will thrive.

And the neighbours, the Murphys, just can't decide whether having the Rumpels next door is the best or the worst thing that ever happened to them.

ISBN 0-88899-036-7 $5.95 paperback

Starring Quincy Rumpel

About to enter grade seven, Quincy Rumpel is determined that this is the year she will make her mark on the world and become a star. As Mr. Rumpel tries to market his latest business venture, the Rumpel Rebounders, Quincy embarks on a grand plan to advertise the rebounders on television and ensure stardom for herself at the same time.

In this sequel to the enormously popular *Quincy Rumpel*, the whole eccentric clan is back in the rambling house at 57 Tulip Street—Leah, Morris, Mr. and Mrs. Rumpel, cousin Gwen and the Murphys. They are joined by crazy Auntie Fan Twistle and Quincy's latest heart-throb, Morris's soccer coach, Desmond.

ISBN 0-88899-048-0 $5.95 paperback

Quincy Rumpel, P.I.

Why is Quincy Rumpel creeping around the old Beanblossom house? Has she discovered the bizarre burial ground of the little dog, Nanki-poo? And what are the strange apparitions that her brother, Morris, sees in the house at night? How about the treasure that Captain Beanblossom left behind? And, most important, who else is interested in the abandoned house?

Quincy Rumpel is back again with an all-woman private investigating firm. But her best-laid plans soon go astray when she's joined by ever-bothersome Morris, his best friend, Chucky, and her heart-throb, Freddie Twikenham, who is convinced that he has his grandfather's Mountie blood coursing through his veins.

ISBN 0-88899-081-2 $5.95 paperback

Morris Rumpel and the Wings of Icarus

Morris Rumpel, youngest member of the crazy and unpredictable Rumpel family, is on his way to the sleepy little town of Cranberry Corners to visit his grandparents for the summer. The trip brings surprises and adventures, from Morris's first airplane flight as an Unaccompanied Minor, to his attempts to learn to ride Fireweed (a horse with a mind of her own!), and a friendship with a family of peregrine falcons that live near his grandparent's farm.

But the vacation turns out to hold more adventure than even Morris has bargained for. It begins the moment he is followed off the plane by a mysterious, icicle-eyed stranger, and the plot thickens as Morris gradually realizes that his new friends, the falcons, are in deadly danger . . .

ISBN 0-88899-099-5 $5.95 paperback

Quincy Rumpel and the Sasquatch of Phantom Cove

It all starts the day the Rumpels receive an invitation to visit their dear friends, Bert and Ernie, at their new fishing resort on the west coast. As Quincy and her family happily pack up the old stationwagon with beach gear, fishing poles and their trusty dog, Snowflake, they imagine lazy summer days spent lying on the dock, fishing and eating fresh salmon in the resort dining room.

But more than one mystery awaits them. The resort is a rundown dump, the Rumpels are the only guests, and there are no fish! When Quincy, Leah and Morris set out to discover why the fish have so mysteriously disappeared they find signs of a very odd creature—a creature that looks a lot like a sasquatch!

ISBN 0-88899-129-0 $6.95 paperback